SPRING FEVER
at
SILVER STREET
FARM

SPRING FEVER
at
SILVER STREET
FARM

NICOLA DAVIES
illustrated by Katharine McEwen

**WALKER
BOOKS**

First published 2011 by Walker Books Ltd
87 Vauxhall Walk, London SE11 5HJ

4 6 8 10 9 7 5 3

This book has been typeset in Stempel Schneidler and Cows

Printed and bound in Great Britain
by Clays Ltd, St Ives plc

British Library Cataloguing in Publication Data:
a catalogue record for this book is available from the British Library

ISBN 978-1-4063-2306-1

www.walker.co.uk

For Joseph and Gabriel,
Sean, the Buffys and the Tea Cosy Hens.

A MAP OF SILVER STREET FARM

FLORA'S OFFICE

Main gate

FLORA'S VAN

Goats

Sheep

gate

Duck House

N

CANAL

Chapter One

Flora, the manager of Silver Street Farm, knew she had to leave; her father had broken his leg and needed her help back on their family farm. But actually leaving the city farm was *very* hard. She had been sitting half in and half out of her van for ten minutes now.

"Och, dear!" she exclaimed, her Scots accent even stronger than usual. "Are you *sure* you'll be OK?"

Meera, Karl and Gemma, the three children who had started Silver Street Farm, tried to reassure her.

"We'll be fine!" said Meera, doing her best to sound as convincing as possible.

"We've got Squirt and Bish Bosh to help," said Gemma.

"I will be here, also," added Karl's Auntie Nat in her strong Russian accent. She had rushed to Silver Street to be the "supervising adult" so Flora could leave.

"It's only for a few days, isn't it?" said Gemma, managing to keep the worry out of her voice.

"Oh, yes!" said Flora. "Just until my brother gets home at the weekend. But it's such bad timing..."

"No, it's *good* timing..." said Karl, doing

the best job of all of them at sounding calm. "It's half-term this week, so we can *all* be here, *all* of the time."

"But I'll miss the Lonchester Cheese Show tomorrow!" Flora complained.

"Don't worry about that, Flora. You've left me instructions about what to do," said Meera, hoping she sounded confident.

Flora was still looking worried.

"But all the animals!" she said anxiously. "They're about to give birth any day now and I haven't finished making new homes for them all!"

"But you're always saying how you can never be absolutely sure when babies will be born," Karl reassured her.

"And they all might be late!" Meera chipped in.

"*We* can finish making new pens for the mums and babies," said Gemma, as brightly as possible.

Flora smiled back at last. "You'll be fine, won't you?" she said.

The children nodded and exchanged a quick phew-we've-convinced-her look.

"Right, then," said Flora, putting both feet in the van for the first time. "The sooner I go, the sooner I'll be back. Where's that dog of mine? Flinty! *Flinty!*"

Flinty the sheepdog came waddling across the yard and clambered over Flora's lap to take her place in the passenger seat.

"Goodness!" exclaimed Flora. "She's getting heavy! Diet for you when we get back, my girl!"

Flora slammed the van door shut and started the engine.

"I don't know why I'm worrying," she said through the window. "This is your farm, after all. See you at the weekend!"

Shading their eyes against the bright spring sunshine, Auntie Nat and the children smiled and waved as Flora pulled away and disappeared into the traffic at the end of the road.

Then Auntie Nat turned to the children with her hands on her hips. "Now you tell me truths," she said. "You *really* think we'll be fine?"

"Well..." said Gemma, "Bish Bosh has been grounded and Squirt's got such a crush on Meera that he can't do anything but wander around after her like a shadow."

"Yeah," said Meera, shaking her head in disapproval. "And the only grown-up who's free this week is you, Auntie Nat."

"But the *really* bad news is that I don't think the piglets are going to be at all late," said Karl. "In fact, I'm pretty sure that at least one litter will be born today."

There was a short pause when no one said a thing. Then Auntie Nat spoke. "OK," she said. "You go look at pigs. I make tea. Also biscuits."

Chapter Two

Mrs Fattybot, one of Silver Street's two Gloucester Old Spot sows, was feeling most peculiar. All morning, she'd been gathering mouthfuls of straw into a big pile, while her tummy was jumping about in a very uncomfortable way. It was all most upsetting. In fact, it was *so* upsetting that, at the exact moment the children opened the gate of her little yard, Mrs Fattybot suddenly felt that she couldn't tolerate her sty for another moment. She shot through the open gate like a fat, spotted missile, knocking the children to one side.

Leaving her sty behind made Mrs Fattybot feel much calmer. She stopped and looked around her. On one side were the old station waiting rooms, where the goats and sheep lived and the hay was stored. On the other was the building that had once been the ticket office and was now the Silver Street Farm office. In between was the yard, which was paved with bricks and dotted with bantam hens. The little turquoise caravan that was Flora's home stood at the far end.

It was a familiar scene that Mrs Fattybot had seen through the bars of the pigsty gate every day since coming to live at Silver Street Farm. But standing in the middle of it suddenly made her feel very nervous. There was so much space all around her and so much sky above her. She turned a little, thinking that perhaps her sty wasn't so bad after all, and saw the three children walking towards her in a rather unfriendly way. If Mrs Fattybot had been human, she would have burst into tears, but, as she was a pig, she ran. Her ears flapped like pink napkins and her tummy wobbled like a giant strawberry blancmange. She sped to the caravan and scrambled in through the open door.

It was cool and shady inside and, once she had pushed through the cramped kitchen and into the living room, there was plenty of floor space. Mrs Fattybot turned around a few times, snuffling approvingly at the rug under her feet. Suddenly, she felt quite at home. There were plenty of things to make a bed with, all much nicer than prickly straw. Mrs Fattybot took several big mouthfuls of clothes and cushions, pushed them into a comfy mound on the floor and lay down with a contented sigh.

The children watched with a mixture of horror and fascination through the gaps in the caravan's curtains as Mrs Fattybot set about wrecking Flora's caravan.

"We have to get her out of there!" said Meera.

"We can't," said Karl. "She could farrow at any moment..."

"She could *what*?" said Meera.

"Farrow – that means have her babies," Karl explained. "When sows start acting like this – wanting to be on their own and making a nest – it means that they are about to give birth to their piglets."

"But we can't let her have babies in Flora's lounge!" Meera almost squealed.

"Actually," Karl said thoughtfully, "Flora loves her pigs so much she might not mind."

"But look what Mrs Fattybot's done to the cushions and the rug!" Meera said.

"Moving her won't get the stain out of the rug or put feathers back in those cushions." Karl said.

"Guys," said Gemma. "I think it's too late anyway... Look!"

Three noses pressed against the caravan's window as the first of Mrs Fattybot's piglets plopped into the world on top of one of Flora's tapestry cushions.

"Wow!" said Meera. "They're so teeny!"

"Just look at their little feet!" said Gemma. "They're so cute!"

"Oh!" Meera gasped, "here comes another one!"

"How many will there be, Karl?" asked Gemma.

"Could be as many as sixteen," he replied.

"Awww," the girls sighed together.

Karl was not about to go as gooey as Meera and Gemma, but he had to admit that the piglets were really very sweet. Almost as soon as they popped out, they tottered on wobbly little legs to their mum's belly to find a teat. In what seemed like just a few minutes, there were three little ginger, spotty piglets lined up by Mrs Fattybot's tummy.

"Well," said Karl at last, "there's not much we can do about Flora's caravan now!"

Meera tore her eyes away from the growing row of little piglets. She realized that Karl was right. They had to get on with all the other jobs that needed doing.

"OK," she said. "Watching piglets being born isn't helping me get ready for the cheese show tomorrow, so I'd better head to the dairy."

"I'll stay here to make sure all the piglets are born safely," said Karl.

"OK," said Meera. "But if you're on piglet duty and I'm on cheeses…"

Karl finished Meera's sentence. "That means Gemma has to do everything else!"

Meera and Karl turned worried faces to their friend, but she was already halfway across the yard.

"No worries!" Gemma called. "It's just feeding and watering. Nothing complicated like being a piggy-midwife!"

Chapter Three

Gemma almost skipped across the yard. It was exciting to be doing farm jobs on her own, without Flora or even Karl or Meera to help. She made a list of chores in her head as she went: feed the turkeys, chickens and ducks; collect any eggs; clean their drinkers and give the birds fresh water; split a hay bale and give some to the sheep and some to the goats; check their water too.

It wasn't a long list, but the turkeys,

chickens and ducks all had different food and their drinkers had to be carried from their pens, which were in three different parts of the farm, to the tap outside Flora's office, and then carried back, full of water and very heavy. The hay bales were big, awkward and hard to handle, fine when there were two pairs of hands to help, but tricky for one. And there was a lot more to think about: Flora had always told the children of the importance of looking carefully at all the livestock whenever the animals were fed or watered. "Anything out of the ordinary, anything at all, could be the first sign of a problem. So keep your eyes *peeled*!"

Flora's voice was going round and round in Gemma's head so much that she managed to pour water from a drinker down the inside of one boot as she checked on the turkeys. The turkeys gobbled nervously as she stood on one leg to empty out her boot.

"Huh," thought Gemma, "just as daft and nervous as always."

Next, Gemma squelched to the chickens. They were scratching in their pen around the old signal box that was their house. They rushed towards Gemma in mad flurry of feathers, like old-fashioned ladies running along in frilly skirts. They pecked and pushed around her feet, all looking sleek and bright-eyed.

Gemma climbed the wooden ladder to the signal box to collect the eggs. There were lots of them – lovely deep brown ones with tiny freckles, chalk-white ones and, Gemma's favourites, the pale blue eggs laid by the Araucana hens. She peered into the gloom at the far end of the house to check on Fluff, the big Silkie chicken who was sitting on a clutch of eggs that were due to hatch very soon. But Fluff wasn't there (in fact, at that moment she was out in the yard pulling a reluctant worm from its hole). Sean, the little white bantam cockerel, was sitting on Fluff's clutch instead. He clucked defiantly at Gemma.

"It's all right, Sean. I'm not going to move you," Gemma whispered. "But what are *you* doing sitting on Fluff's eggs?"

A broody cockerel – now, that was definitely out of the ordinary! But there was no time to think about that now … there were still the ducks, the sheep and the goats to attend to!

Gemma loved the ducks, especially as she had hatched some of them herself from eggs that had been thrown away for being "rotten". Right now, the ducks were preening on the small jetty that allowed them to get in and out of the canal without having to jump from the top of a high wall. They tucked into their feed of mash, making the quiet little quacks of pleasure that sounded to Gemma like duck gossip.

Everything seemed fine. But, when Gemma checked inside the duck house for eggs, she found Buster, the farm guard dog, lying on the floor sniffing at a pile of broken shells!

Gemma felt as if an old friend had been revealed as a wicked criminal. It was clear that Buster had sneaked in and eaten the eggs.

"Oh, Buster!" she said. "Whatever made you do that?" And Buster wagged his tail as if he'd done nothing wrong at all.

"You come with me!" Gemma told him sternly and Buster followed her meekly across the yard. Gemma shut him in the office, then headed off to tend to the sheep.

Bitzi and Bobo, the two Shetland ewes who had started their careers as Auntie Nat's poodles, really *were* fine. They pulled hungrily at the net of hay Gemma hung on the fence for them and leaned into her hand as she scratched the tops of their woolly heads. They were definitely looking pregnant now. Bobo was especially huge and from the back looked almost as wide as she was long. But there were no signs that either of them was about to give birth any time soon.

Phew, Gemma thought. *Glad there's nothing to worry about there!*

She staggered across the farm with a bucket of clean water for the goats, thinking sadly of Buster's egg stealing and Sean the cockerel sitting on Fluff's clutch of eggs. Would Silver Street *ever* have its own chicks or ducklings?

"Well, at least Bitzi and Bobo are OK," she thought. "And the goats are never any trouble."

But when Gemma reached the goat house, she found that, quietly and without giving anyone any trouble at all, one of the goats had given birth to twins! Two gorgeous little brown and white kids nestled in the straw at their mum's feet.

Chapter Four

Meera always felt that she should whisper in the dairy. It was sort of *holy*. The walls were painted white and everything was made of stainless steel. There was never a speck of dirt anywhere. You had to wear special clothes: white overalls, a hairnet and white boots, all spotlessly clean.

The dairy was where the fresh milk from the Silver Street nanny goats – which would spoil and go off in just a day or two – was turned into cheese that would last and last, storing up the goodness of the milk for months. The whole process seemed quite magical to Meera.

The goats had stopped giving milk about two months back, halfway through their pregnancies, but all the milk they'd produced up until then had been turned into cheese. Rows of cheeses sat on the dairy's cool shelves, "ripening" and getting tastier by the day. But they didn't do it on their own; they had to be turned twice a day and cleaned of any nasty moulds. Finally, just before they were ready to be sold and eaten, the cheeses were rolled in "Flora's Secret Formula" – a special mixture of herbs, salt and other Top Secret ingredients.

Flora always said that you had to be "steady and predictable" to milk goats and make cheese; and, although these were the last words anyone would have used to describe Meera, she loved helping with the milking and cheesemaking. So, when Flora had asked her to be in charge of the cheeses while she was away, Meera had actually blushed with pleasure.

Being "in charge" included preparing ten cheeses for the Lonchester Cheese Show, to be entered for the Big Cheese trophy. Now, standing in her hairnet, white boots and overalls, Meera felt nervous. She'd never actually seen Flora give the cheeses their Secret Formula overcoat, and Flora had left in such a hurry that all she'd had time to do was scribble some instructions on a piece of paper.

Meera took a deep breath and laid Flora's list of instructions out in front of her.

1. Loose ten best chickens from toastelf.

"Flora's handwriting's terrible," said Meera to herself. "It's a good thing I know that she really means: 'Choose the ten best cheeses from the top shelf'."

But the next instructions were a little harder to understand. It looked like Flora was telling Meera to:

2. *Help axe over loo seat.*

3. *Saint axe oven chickens.*

4. *Loll in Sweet Family hen fill eat.*

"Chickens" had to be "cheeses" and "Sweet Family" must mean "Secret Formula", but what was "axe"? And what did "loo seat" really mean?

"Hello!" said a small voice.

Meera looked up. Squirt stood on the other side of the metal table, his head only just visible above it, his body and legs lost inside big white overalls and boots. He was holding something behind his back and nervously shifting from one foot to the other.

Meera sighed. The last thing she needed was Squirt hanging about and getting in the way. "Squirt," she said. "I'm a bit busy right now."

Squirt's face fell as he realized that he was about to be sent away.

"I can't read Flora's handwriting, so I can't work out what I need to do to these cheeses!" Meera explained.

Squirt brightened immediately. "I know what you do," he said. "You paint 'em with wax."

"How do you know that?" asked Meera.

"It says so on your instructions," said Squirt, nodding towards the sheet of paper in front of Meera.

"How can you read this from over there?" she asked, puzzled.

"My social worker's got much worse

handwriting than Flora – and I'm always reading what he writes upside down!"

Squirt's grin was infectious and Meera laughed. If he could read Flora's writing, Squirt really *might* be useful.

"Number two says, 'Melt wax over low heat'," Squirt read, coming round to Meera's side of the table. "Then number three says, 'Paint wax over cheeses', and the last one says, 'Roll in Secret Formula when still wet'!"

"Squirt," said Meera, "you are a genius!"

Squirt went so pink, he glowed.

"Can you tip the Secret Formula out onto the table, while I melt the wax?" Meera asked him.

Without even replying, Squirt snatched up the box of Secret Formula and tipped its entire contents onto the table. Unfortunately, the bunch of flowers that he had been holding behind his back, ready to present to Meera, rather got in the way. So when Meera turned round, ready with brush, melted wax and her first cheese, Flora's Secret Formula had some extra ingredients: hundreds of little orange and blue petals, and thousands of yellow blobs of pollen. Squirt's face was white.

"I'm s-s-s-s-so s-s-s-sorry, Meera," he gulped. "I brought the flowers for you and…"

Sometimes, Meera decided, with cheese-making it was good *not* to be "steady" or "predictable", because sometimes you just had to cope with the wobbly unpredictableness of life. "Well," she said, suppressing a sigh, "this batch of cheeses will just have to look a bit different."

"Even if," she added quietly to herself, "that means not winning any prizes…"

Chapter Five

The spring nights were still chilly, so the children were glad to sit around the fire in the Silver Street Farm office, tucking into the food that Auntie Nat had brought with her. With Karl's auntie at Silver Street as "supervising adult" the children could spend the night on the farm. This was something they hardly ever got to do, but it was essential while Flora was away.

Auntie Nat might not have been able to

tell a poodle from a lamb, but she was a great cook. Karl, Meera and Gemma always loved her food and tonight she had cooked their favourite things: potato latkes and her very best chocolate cake for afters. But not even this meal could cheer them up. They ate so quietly that the only sound was Buster gently snoring in front of the fire.

"So," Auntie Nat said brightly. "A good day, no? Those little piggies were super cute eh? And so many! And the baby goats ... awww!"

"Yes," said Karl. "Fourteen piglets. But it's wrecked Flora's caravan..."

"...and we've nowhere else to put them..."

"...and no separate pens ready for the nannies and their kids..."

"...and we're never going to get any chicks or ducklings..."

"...and the cheeses won't win a prize..."

From being so very quiet, suddenly the children couldn't stop talking. All their worries poured out.

"Stop, stop, *stop*!" said Auntie Nat, holding up her hands. "Your first day 'solo' and you have got so gloomy? This is not the three kids I know. The three kids *I* know started this farm and they are never defeated, yes?"

The children nodded.

"Now," said Auntie Nat, "you eat more cake and we solve all problems. OK?"

"OK," the children replied quietly together.

"The big problem is you need more pairs of hands," said Auntie Nat. "So tomorrow, I will get you helping hands. No questions. I will just do it. With hands you can make new pens for babies, yes?"

The children nodded again.

"Eggs. This is more tricky. You need incubator. On Internet, you find all things. Poodles that are sheeps, for instance. So incubator is easy."

Yet again the children nodded.

"And as for this dog," Auntie Nat went on, kneeling beside Buster, "I am powerful psychic, OK? This dog is no thief. You wait and see if what I say not true."

Chapter Six

Long after the children had gone to sleep, Auntie Nat had been busy on her mobile, having conversations in at least three different languages. The results of her efforts stood at the door of the Silver Street Farm office at nine the next morning: three of the most extraordinary-looking ladies the children had ever seen. They were wearing jeans and wellington boots ready for farm work, but their top halves were clothed in garments that seemed to have come from a dressing-up box.

"Here," Auntie Nat announced proudly, "are your helping hands."

The three ladies smiled and inclined their jewel-encrusted, scarf-wrapped, hat-topped heads in three little bows to the children.

"I introduce you," Auntie Nat continued. "First, this is Madame Arkady" she said, presenting a thin woman in a sequin-covered top with strings of pearls wound into her dark hair. "You want to speak with dead relatives, she fix."

Madame Arkady smiled modestly, then added in a French accent, "Also, I grew up on a farm in Normandy."

"Next, Miss Zelda!" said Auntie Nat, turning to a large red-headed lady in a green satin blouse and matching beret. "The best reader of minds in Europe."

"Alzo," added Miss Zelda, "zee daughter of dairy farmer near Heidelberg."

"And, last but not least," smiled Auntie Nat, "Miss Blanche Berkley, the queen of all palm readers."

Blanche tipped her white Stetson at the children and shook their hands. "Yep, that's me. You can take the girl outta Texas, but you can't take Texas outta the girl. Leastways, not the cattle-ranching part!"

Astonished, the children stared at Auntie Nat's "helping hands".

"I have got to be dreaming!" whispered Karl.

"Well, I'm dreaming the same dream then," said Meera.

"Me too," breathed Gemma.

Miss Zelda rummaged in the bag of tools at her feet.

"Shall vee begin?" she enquired.

"We understand," said Madame Arkady, pulling a pair of gardening gloves over her perfectly manicured hands, "that you need to build some new pens for *les bébés, non*?"

"And the one thing gals who grew up on farms know all about," grinned Miss Blanche, "is makin' fences and homes for critters!"

Auntie Nat and Meera watched Karl and Gemma leading the ladies across the yard toward the goat house.

Meera sighed. "I wish I was going to be here today instead of at the Cheese Show."

"Ah!" said Auntie Nat mysteriously. "I think you enjoy big cheese party more than you think!"

"Yeah," said Squirt popping up from nowhere, like he always seemed to do. "Especially with me there to help!"

Chapter Seven

Buster lay in the sunshine by the Silver Street gates. His eyes were half-closed and he looked almost asleep. But he wasn't. Buster was on duty, busy guarding, and alert to all that was going on around him. He could hear Meera and Squirt loading the cheeses into Auntie Nat's car; he could hear wire being unrolled down in the goat pen; he could hear and smell the three new grown-up humans. He could tell that Meera was nervous and that Gemma was still a bit cross.

Gemma was cross about what had happened in the duck house. Buster understood this; he was cross himself, but surprised that a mere human would be clever enough to work out what had been going on. Gemma must have a nose just like a dog, he decided, to know about the wicked creature that had been stealing the duck eggs. Even now, in broad daylight, he could pick up a faint hint of the creature's sharp smell. It drifted up from the water's edge, fine as a thread of hair at first, then thicker until it was a fat rope of musky stink … it was getting closer! With a deep growl in his throat, Buster got to his feet and raced towards the duck house.

The creature was certainly bold. Buster could smell, and now even hear that it was inside the duck house, doing its wickedness. But the gate down to the ducks' jetty and ramp was shut tight! Buster barked and growled, jumped up and scrabbled at the gate with his big paws, but by the time he'd pushed through the gate and run down to the ramp, scattering the ducks in all directions, the creature was gone, leaving empty shells once more.

Buster was growling over them when Karl and Gemma arrived. Gemma seemed even crosser than she had been before. To Buster's astonishment, Karl was cross as well, and Buster wondered if Karl also had a better nose than he had given him credit for.

Both children shouted and made stern faces, and Buster wagged his tail at them to try to show that he would catch the creature next time. But when they pulled him away by the collar, Buster began to doubt that the humans really understood at all.

Meanwhile, up in the chicken house, Sean the bantam cockerel was also confused. The old signal box might look like a fine place for chickens, but why didn't the humans realize that there were terrible draughts blowing up from between its floorboards? He could feel one now, working its way under his feathers like a cold claw. No wonder Fluffy had given up – not even the broodiest, most motherly of hens would sit on eggs with a cold breeze blowing under her bottom! So even though sitting on eggs was hens' work, Sean crouched lower over them and did what he could to keep them warm.

Chapter Eight

Meera had to admit that Squirt really *was* pretty useful. He'd helped her carry the heavy box of cheeses up the big marble steps of the city hall and found the Silver Street Farm stall among the many others at the Lonchester Cheese Show.

Now, at last, their stall was ready. The cheeses were laid out, with one sliced into bite-sized bits for people to taste, and leaflets about Silver Street Farm were arranged in neat little piles. The only thing that was missing was some visitors.

Meera stared out into the dense crowd of people. No one was even *looking* their way. Somehow, she had to get people's attention. But how was anyone going to notice one girl in this crowd? It was, Meera decided suddenly, all a matter of height.

She put a large box on the table, then put the stool she had been sitting on on top of the box. She put the leaflet box on top of that and then began to climb.

"What are you doing?" Squirt hissed from down near her feet.

"Getting us some attention," replied Meera. "Watch!"

Meera stood on the topmost box and

cleared her throat, ready for her best public speaking voice.

"Ladies and gentlemen!" she shouted, "Roll up, roll up!"

People began to turn around, nudging each other and pointing at the girl balanced on a wobbly tower of boxes and furniture. Meera saw all the faces turned towards her; it was working!

"Come and sample the amazing – the amazing – *flowery* cheese from Lonchester's first and only city farm at Silver Street!" Meera announced, but just as the words "Silver Street" left her mouth, her wobbly tower toppled over, pitching into a sea of rather surprised cheese lovers.

"Well," said Squirt, as the St John's Ambulance volunteer finished putting Meera's arm in a sling, "that certainly got everyone's attention. Especially the judges you landed on."

Meera groaned. "Did anyone come to the stall after I fell?"

"Are you kidding?" grinned Squirt, "I was rushed off my feet! There's not a bit of cheese or a single leaflet left."

Meera brightened up.

"What about the judges?"

Squirt's smile disappeared. He scratched his ear.

"They weren't too bright after being flattened," he said. "But they *did* come and taste our cheese, so I suppose we've got *some* chance."

The Tannoy on the wall above Meera and Squirt crackled into life.

"Ladies and gentlemen," said the announcer's voice. "Here is the news you've all been waiting for – the winner of this year's Big Cheese Cup. The judges were quite united in their choice. This year the prize goes to … Silver Street Farm, for their Flowery Goats' Cheese!"

"Goodness me!" said the St John's Ambulance lady to Meera. "If you jump about like that, your bandage is going to come right off!"

Chapter Nine

"Names are so important. You've got to find the right one," Gemma was explaining to Madame Arkady and Miss Zelda as they released the goats into their new, improved and much bigger pens. "We didn't find the right names for the goats before today."

"Vell," said Miss Zelda, smiling at Madame Arkady. "Vee are honoured that you name zee Silver Street goats after us."

"*C'est super!*" exclaimed Madame Arkady. "*C'est formidable!* I think Arkady is the perfect name for the brown one with droopy ears…"

"And zee white one, I think she knows her name already!" Miss Zelda said. "Zelda! Zelda!"

The Saanen looked up from her hay and her twin kids said "meeek" as if they really did recognize their mum's name.

"Ah!" said Miss Zelda, cocking her head as if she had just heard a voice. "Vee are needed by Karl and Blanche. It is time vee move zee piggies."

"Oh!" said Karl, smiling and a little surprised. "I was just coming to get you!"

"Yep," said Miss Blanche, pushing her Stetson back on her head. "We need all hands for moving Miss Fattybot and her young 'uns here. But then," she said, winking at Miss Zelda, "I guess y'all knew that already, right?"

Everyone peered in through the window of Flora's caravan. What had been Flora's neat little living room was now, quite literally, a pigsty. The piglets were asleep in a heap on a nest of sheets and blankets and Mrs Fattybot was contentedly stretched out on Flora's ruined sofa cushions.

"Sure has made herself at home," Miss Blanche commented.

"Hmmm," said Gemma. "How are we going to persuade her to get out of there?"

"Food," replied Karl. "I haven't fed her at all today, so she must be hungry. My guess is that the moment she hears a food bucket being rattled by the door, she'll be out here like a rocket. Then she *should* just follow where the bucket goes."

"Our job," Miss Blanche told Miss Zelda with a grin, "is steering. We'll fence her in along the way with these bits of board until she gets to her new home." Miss Blanche tipped her head towards the rather eccentric extension to the pig sty that was just visible behind a wall on the other side of the yard.

"And *les bébés*?" Madame Arkady enquired, raising one of her perfect black eyebrows. "They are too small to follow, no?"

"That's where you and Gemma come in," said Karl, warming to his master plan. "You nip inside the caravan, pop the piglets into this barrow and wheel them to the new pen."

"See, we have it all ready, cosied up with straw!" said Miss Blanche.

"OK!" said Karl. "Everyone ready?"

Miss Blanche and Miss Zelda stood by with the boards, while Madame Arkady and Gemma grinned at each other, rather looking forward to their job of piglet-napping. Then Karl opened the caravan door and began to rattle the bucket of food.

Mrs Fattybot loved her new home. It was especially suitable for her piglets, being so warm. But today, the young male human – of whom she was rather fond because he always scratched exactly the right spot on her back – had failed to bring her breakfast. Didn't he know what hungry work it was making enough milk for fourteen piglets?

She was just thinking that she should go out and find something to eat on her own, when she heard the best sound in all the world: the rattling of pig pellets in the bottom of a bucket. Instantly, Mrs Fattybot's mouth began to water. She struggled to her feet with a grunt and stumped out through the caravan kitchen to the front door. She hardly even noticed the boards held up on either side of the entrance. All she saw, heard and smelled (mmmmm!) was that bucket and its *delicious* contents. But every time she moved forward, the bucket seemed to move away. It was most annoying.

Then, from behind her, Mrs Fattybot heard her babies squeaking in distress. Forgetting all about the food she turned around, pushing the walls out of her way, and saw her precious piglets, being stolen by two humans! Mrs Fattybot's brain filled with pure fury. She screamed so loudly that the panes of glass in the Silver Street Farm office shivered. And then she charged.

Chapter Ten

Meera and Squirt were in high spirits. They'd run into two old friends at the Lonchester Cheese Show: Sashi and Stewy, who were from Cosmic TV, and had helped to tell the citizens of Lonchester all about Silver Street Farm right from the start. Today they'd been sent to cover the story of the Big Cheese Cup winner and were delighted to find that they would be interviewing and filming old buddies from Silver Street. Sashi had decided that the story needed shots of the dairy and the goats, so they all piled into Stewy's van and headed for Silver Street Farm, with Meera telling the Cosmic TV crew about how well organized everything was going to be at the city farm now, with lots of nice new pens for all the new babies.

But when they got to Silver Street Farm, it was chaos. Mrs Fattybot was in the middle of the yard charging at any human who came within range, and Gemma, Karl and the three ladies were running around as if they were demented. And there were tiny ginger and black spotted piglets *everywhere*.

"Hey!" said Stewy with a big grin. "Little pig dudes. Wicked!"

*　　*　　*

At last, the piglets were rounded up and they and their excitable mum were safely inside their new sty next door to Mojo. Mrs Fattybot grunted at her old friend through the fence, probably recounting what a terrible day she'd had.

All the Silver Streeters leant over the wall of the sty watching Mrs Fattybot's fourteen "young 'uns" lined up along their mum's tummy, suckling happily.

"Oh, those piglets!" crooned Sashi and Miss Zelda as one.

"Yes!" added Madame Arkady. "They are so sweet!"

"How come they ain't the same colour as their ma, Karl?" asked Miss Blanche. "They're kinda the colour of Zelda's hair!"

"Their dad was a Tamworth, which is a

ginger breed," said Karl. "So they're Gloucester-Old-Spot-Tamworth crosses. They're supposed to be good for bacon."

"How can you say that, dude?" said Stewy, shocked. "Piggies, cover your ears!"

"The baby goats are sweet," said Sashi, "but these are just divine. We'll come back in the morning when the light's better to get some shots. I want these on tomorrow's local news!"

"Ah!" said Miss Zelda. "Piggies on TV. Many visitors at the weekend, I think!"

"Oh, yeah," Sashi added as she and Stewy got into the car. "And there's one more thing. I think that by tomorrow morning, I may have a solution for Flora's wrecked caravan!"

Chapter Eleven

The Helping Hands stayed on to help with all the evening chores, and when Auntie Nat called to say that she would be late, Miss Blanche went and got pizzas for everyone. As the sun set, they all sat around the fire drinking tea and nibbling on the last bits of pizza crust.

"Thank you so much for all your help today," said Meera to the three ladies.

"You know what?" said Miss Zelda. "I knew you were going to say zat!"

"No need for thanks," said Madame Arkady. "I've had the most fun!"

"Me also," Miss Zelda smiled. "The animals here are so lovely!" She slipped the last bit of her pizza to Buster, who was leaning against her leg.

"Don't," said Gemma. "He's in disgrace. We think he's been eating the duck eggs."

"Really?" Miss Zelda looked down at Buster as if asking him for his side of the story. "No," she said, shaking her head. "This dog is not a thief. He's a hero. You let him out. He will show you."

"Now?" asked Gemma.

"Yes, now," said Miss Zelda. "But we must be quiet and follow."

Meera, Karl and Gemma glanced at one another; it was all a bit weird. But then the whole *day* had been weird…

"Why not?" said Karl.

"We've nothing to lose, really," said Meera.

Gemma nodded and let Buster out into the night.

Buster set off at a trot across the darkened yard, followed by Meera, Gemma and Karl. When they reached the gate to the ducks' pen, Gemma silently slid the bolt and Buster slipped inside like a shadow. As quietly as he could, he padded to the edge of the jetty and stood waiting.

Buster cocked his head as he heard a tiny *plop*. Something had dropped into the water on the other side of the canal. Something was coming his way. He crouched low to keep out of sight. He would just have to hope it wouldn't notice his smell amid the scent of duck droppings! A tiny breath; it had surfaced halfway across the canal. Buster's heart raced. This time, *this time* he would get it!

The children and the ladies stood at the gate to the duck pen, straining their eyes and ears in the darkness. There was nothing, just the pool of dark and quiet that surrounded Silver Street, and the noise and light of the city beyond. No one dared speak. The moments seemed to stretch like elastic. Then suddenly there was a growl, a kind of cat-like yowl and a huge splash.

"Quick!" said Karl. "Who's got the torch?"

"Me!" said Gemma, flicking it on and shining a beam of light down onto the duck jetty. There was no sign of Buster.

The jetty wouldn't take everyone's weight and Miss Blanche insisted that the children stay back from the water in the dark. Instead, she went forward and shone the torch onto the water. For what seemed like ages there was nothing – not a sound, not a ripple. And then suddenly in the beam there was Buster, struggling to swim with a dead mink gripped in his jaws. The egg thief had been caught at last.

Chapter Twelve

"I tell you Buster is a hero!" said Auntie Nat, fussing Buster's velvety ears and feeding him toast. "I tell you, but you don't listen to me! Huh!"

But she wasn't really cross. Nobody could be cross on such an amazing morning, with the sun shining on the new pens and the new baby animals, and the crew of the DIY makeover programme that Sashi and Stewy had brought with them when they arrived!

"The house they were going to do up fell through," Sashi said.

"Fell down, actually," Stewy chipped in.

"And the producer's an old buddy of mine," Sashi added. "He called me to see if I could think of a replacement location…"

"So now," said Stewy grinning, "they can do up the loft above the office before Flora gets back. Then she'll have a new flat!"

The sound of banging and sawing came down through the ceiling.

"Let's go and see the pigs," said Stewy. "It's way too noisy in here."

As Karl and the Cosmic TV duo headed out to the pigsty, Meera went to the dairy to give the cheeses their daily turn.

Squirt went along to help because, as he said, "Even Meera can't wrangle cheeses with one hand!"

Gemma stayed amidst the noise and banging in the farm office, making as much fuss of Buster as she could to make up for having doubted him.

"Everyone has what they want, yes?" said Auntie Nat. "Meera has big cheese prize and Karl has piglets. But what about you, Gemma?" she asked, looking at Gemma over the rim of her coffee cup.

"Well, I'll get eggs from the ducks now..." said Gemma.

"But you want chicks, yes? Ducklings?"

"Yes, I do."

"Ha!" said Auntie Nat, jumping up. "Look what I got!"

She dragged Gemma to the far end of the office and pulled a blanket from what looked like an old box by the electric socket.

The box was plugged in and had a see-through lid. And inside was a huge white egg.

"An incubator!" exclaimed Gemma, throwing her arms around Auntie Nat. "Now we can hatch chicks even if the hens never become broody!"

"But first," said Auntie Nat, "you hatch this big egg, yes? Man who sold it to me make me promise to hatch it. He says it's ostrich egg."

Gemma lifted the lid of the incubator and put the egg to her ear. It felt warm and alive. Inside was a faint tapping.

"I can hear it tapping, Auntie Nat," she said. "Do you? It's going to hatch soon!"

"Wow!" said Auntie Nat. "Silver Street Ostrich Farm!"

Gemma was about to explain that it wasn't a goose egg, not an ostrich egg, when someone knocked on the office door.

"Hello?" said a very familiar voice. "Anybody home?"

It was Bish Bosh, looking perky and full of mischief.

"Hello, stranger," said Gemma. "You're not grounded any more, then?"

"No, I'm on my best behaviour." Bish Bosh grinned. "But my social worker says that I need someone to keep an eye on me. So I came down here!"

Gemma thought of how the ducklings she had hatched in her bedroom had followed her around like her own shadow. She beamed at Bish Bosh. "In that case," she said, handing him the egg, "I've got just the job for you, Bish Bosh. Pretty soon you could have someone who won't let you out of their sight for a moment!"

Chapter Thirteen

Flora texted Meera, so that everyone at Silver Street Farm would know she was on her way. But she didn't call. She didn't want to know about all the disasters that must be waiting for her. So many things *could* have gone wrong.

So when she turned into the Silver Street Yard on Friday afternoon, Flora couldn't believe her eyes. There were neat new pens, with proper fences and gates; there were curtains hanging at the windows above the office; there was no sign of her horrid old caravan and there was a table in the middle of the yard with the Big Cheese silver cup on top of it!

Flora got out of the van and walked to the table. Her name was engraved on the cup! She blinked and looked at it again, wondering if her long drive from Scotland had sent her potty. Then, with a big cheer, the children, Auntie Nat and a TV film crew burst out of the office, with Buster barking wildly beside them. Now Flora knew she'd gone mad.

"Welcome home! Welcome home!" they all shouted.

The children and the TV crew (who Flora vaguely recognized) led her up a new staircase into a beautiful little bedsit. The room looked just as Flora had always planned it, but she'd never had the time to work on it. There was even a new sofa and all her books were already on the shelves. No more sleeping in that grotty little caravan.

But there wasn't time for Flora to sit about in her new home because the children were desperate to take her out on the farm. All the animals seemed to have had their babies quite happily without her!

The goats now had four kids between them, and all girl babies, which meant that there would be more milk for more cheese; Flora's beloved pigs had had their babies too, gorgeous, wriggling little piglets that she was too dazed to count. When they reached the sheep pen, she was almost surprised that the sheep were still looking very pregnant. *At least somebody waited!* she thought.

Most amazing of all were the two precious chicks being paraded across the pen by dear little Sean. He had actually hatched them.

"Poor wee soul!" Flora breathed. "Oh, dear! I never mended those terrible drafts in the floorboards. I'll do it first thing tomorrow, Sean."

It was all totally overwhelming and Flora was just about to give in to a very un-Flora-like fit of tears when Bish Bosh appeared through the gates followed very, very closely by a grey gosling.

"All right Flora?" he called out, strolling across the yard with his usual swagger. "Hey!" he said, turning to the gosling and grinning. "I'm a responsible family man now."

Instead of crying, Flora laughed and laughed and laughed. And then she remembered that she had a surprise for the children. She led them to the back door of her van.

"Look!" she said. "You're not the only ones with unexpected babies."

There, curled up in the back of the van, in a new, proper dog bed, was Flinty. And with her were four little black and grey puppies.

Meera gasped. "They look just like…"

"Buster!" said Karl and Gemma together.

The Silver Street hero didn't say a thing, just modestly wagged his tail.

SILVER STREET FARM

The Little Farm in the Big City

WELCOME TO SILVER STREET FARM

NICOLA DAVIES

ESCAPE FROM SILVER STREET FARM

NICOLA DAVIES

SPRING FEVER AT SILVER STREET FARM

NICOLA DAVIES

ALL ABOARD AT SILVER STREET FARM

NICOLA DAVIES